Before reading

Look at the book cover
Ask, "What do you think

To build independence, ~~words~~ are not included
at the start of this book. If the child needs extra practice, turn
back to pages 6 and 7 in 11a and read the words again with
the child.

During reading

Offer plenty of support and praise as the child reads the story.
Listen carefully and respond to events in the text.

When a **Key Word** is used for the first time, it is also shown at
the bottom of the page. If the child hesitates over a word, point
to the **New Key Words** box and practise reading it together.
If the word is phonically decodable, you can sound out the
letters and blend the sounds to read the word ("d-o-g, dog").
Praise the child for their effort, then return to the story.

Pause every few pages and ask questions to check the child's
understanding of what they have read. If they begin to lose
concentration, stop reading and save the page for later.

Celebrate the child's achievement and come back to the
story the next day.

After reading

After reading this book, ask, "Did you enjoy the story? What did
you like about it?" Encourage the child to share their opinions.

Use the comprehension questions on page 54 to check the
child's understanding and recall of the text.

Ladybird

Series Consultant: Professor David Waugh
With thanks to Kulwinder Maude

LADYBIRD BOOKS

UK | USA | Canada | Ireland | Australia
India | New Zealand | South Africa

Ladybird Books is part of the Penguin Random House group of companies
whose addresses can be found at global.penguinrandomhouse.com.
www.penguin.co.uk   www.puffin.co.uk   www.ladybird.co.uk

Penguin
Random House
UK

Original edition of Key Words with Peter and Jane first published by Ladybird Books Ltd 1964
Series updated 2023
This book first published 2023
001

With thanks to Liz Pemberton for her contributions in advising on the illustrations
With thanks to Inclusive Minds for connecting us with their Inclusion Ambassador network,
and in particular thanks to Guntaas Kaur Chugh for her input on the illustrations

Printed in China

The authorized representative in the EEA is Penguin Random House Ireland,
Morrison Chambers, 32 Nassau Street, Dublin D02 YH68

A CIP catalogue record for this book is available from the British Library

ISBN: 978-0-241-51104-6

All correspondence to:
Ladybird Books
Penguin Random House Children's
One Embassy Gardens, 8 Viaduct Gardens, London SW11 7BW

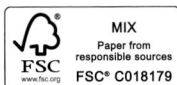

MIX
Paper from
responsible sources
FSC® C018179

Key Words

with Peter and Jane

11b

Adventure World

Based on the original
Key Words with Peter and Jane
reading scheme and research by William Murray

Original edition written by William Murray
This edition written by Abbie Rushton
Illustrated by Martyn Cain
Based on characters and design by Gustavo Mazali

Adventure World had come to the park!

It was Saturday night, and Peter, Jane, Mum and Dad were walking through the park when Tess started barking.

"What's the matter, Tess?" asked Jane.

"She saw something through the trees," Dad said.

"I bet it was a fox," said Peter.
"Or a mouse."

"I hope there won't be rain," said Mum, looking up.

"I don't mind!" said Jane. "That's what raincoats are for."

New Key Words

adventure   world   night   through
fox   mouse   rain

At Adventure World, Jane spotted a poster. "Look!" she said. "A lost dog."

Everyone came over to see.

"He's so little," said Peter.

"His name is Jet," Jane read. "What a sweet name."

"We can look around for him while we're here," Dad said.

"Wow! Look at all the stands!" Peter said, looking around Adventure World. "Look at that rainbow popcorn!"

Lots of people were buying rainbow popcorn from the stand.

New Key Words

| lost | everyone | came | name |
| | around | while | |

Two police said hello to the children as they went by.

"Hello!" Peter shouted. "I'd like to be in the police."

Then, Jane pointed to the rides, shouting, "Let's go on the Runaway Train!"

Mum held Tess's lead while everyone went on the ride.

Suddenly, Tess barked.

"What is it, Tess?" Mum said. Then, Mum thought she saw a black-and-white tail under one of the food stands.

New Key Words

two	police	went	shout
	suddenly	food	

The train bumped, rolled and rocked around.

"Woohoo!" Peter cried.

"Adventure World is amazing!" Jane shouted, throwing her hands in the air. "I'm glad we came!"

"I'm not sure this ride was a good idea," Dad said, looking a bit sick.

As soon as the ride finished, Peter said, "Can we go again?"

"Oh no, no way," Dad said. "That was the one and only time for me! That ride went on far too long."

New Key Words

cried   idea   oh   only   long

Peter and Jane ran back to join Mum. Suddenly, Peter stopped and pointed at a food stand.

"Mum," he said. "I think I just saw a small dog – the lost one!"

Seeing where Peter was pointing, Mum said, "Tess was looking over there. I think she spotted the lost dog too."

"Maybe it wasn't a fox or a mouse Tess saw by those plants while we were walking here," cried Jane. "Maybe it was the lost dog. Clever Tess!"

Everyone went over to the food stand and peered under it, but there was nothing there.

New Key Words

ran   small   plant   nothing

"Do you need some help?" someone asked. The family turned around and saw the police again.

"Oh, yes. We thought we saw the lost dog," said Dad. "We saw a poster when we came in."

"There!" Jane shouted as the dog ran out. Everyone looked.

"He went that way!" said Peter. He shouted the dog's name, but it ran off into the night.

"He'll be back. There's lots of food around here," the policewoman said. "You two go and have some fun. We'll watch out for him."

New Key Words

need　　woman　　watch

"Let's go on the Mouse Run ride," said Jane.

"What about the Sky Swing ride?" asked Dad.

"Or the bumper cars?" asked Peter.

"Yes, bumper cars!" said Mum, handing Tess's lead to Dad.

Jane and Peter went in one car, and Mum went in the other.

"We're going to bump you!" Peter shouted to Mum.

"I've got an idea, Peter," Jane said. "Go around there."

"Look out, you two!" Mum shouted, bumping into the back of them suddenly.

"Can we get some food, Dad?" Peter asked after they left the bumper cars.

"Let's have chips!" Dad said.

Everyone ate the chips from small cones while they watched a man and a woman go into the Spooky Train ride. They could hear cries and shouts coming from inside.

"Listen to that!" Mum said.

Suddenly, a man screamed.

"Can we go on it?" Peter asked.

"NO!" shouted Mum, Dad and Jane.

New Key Words

man   listen

Suddenly, Tess started to bark again. "You can have a chip, Tess," Mum said. "But only one."

"She's watching something around those two bins," Dad said. "It's only a fox or a mouse."

"No, Dad, look!" Jane said. "It's not a fox or a mouse. It's Jet, the lost dog!" Jane called Jet's name louder, but the small dog turned and ran off.

"Come on, everyone!" Mum cried.

"Stop that lost dog!" Dad shouted as they all ran after Jet.

New Key Words

The policeman and the policewoman heard Dad shouting. They came to help, but the small dog ran through the policeman's legs! Then, Jet went through a gap between two food stands. Everyone followed.

"Oh no! We've lost him again," said the policeman.

Peter looked under the food stand. "He's here," Peter said.

Jane came beside Peter. She softly called the dog's name, but he didn't move.

"I've got an idea," Peter said. "We can give him some food." He took out one of his chips.

Slowly, Jet came nearer to Peter. Jane waited until the last moment before she took hold of the small dog. "Got you at last!" she cried.

"He's shivering," said Jane.

Mum took off her raincoat. "Here, use this to keep him snug," she said.

"I'll find the lost dog poster and call the number on it," the policewoman said.

It wasn't long before a man ran up to them.

"Oh, Jet!" the man cried, as Jet licked his hand. "He went missing here last night."

He turned to Peter and Jane. "Thank you so much," he said. "My name is Gurdeep. Jet's the best dog in the world. You've made me very happy. I need to give you a small gift."

"Oh, you don't need to do that," Jane said. "Everyone helped."

Seeing the food stands, the man said, "I will get hot drinks for everyone!"

"Oh, thank you," cried Peter.

New Key Words

made

WIN   PRIZES   WIN   W

"Shall we go on the Sky Swing next?" Peter asked.

"Yes, come on then," Dad said, as he and Peter ran over to it.

Mum and Jane watched while Dad went on the ride with Peter.

"Wheeee!" Peter shouted.

"Oh dear," Dad said suddenly. He looked ill again.

When the two of them came off the ride, Mum looked at her watch. "Listen, only one last ride," she said. "It's been a long night. We need to get home."

Looking around Adventure World, Peter and Jane picked the Big Wheel.

New Key Words

The policeman came and said he could look after Tess while the family all went on the Big Wheel.

Everyone waved to the two police and Tess from the top.

"We're a very long way up!" Peter said.

When they were back on the ground, Jane said, "I think Adventure World is the best funfair in the country!"

"Not just the country – the world!" Peter cried.

Looking up at the night sky, Dad said, "I think it's going to rain soon. Let's go home."

New Key Words

country

33

As they left, the family thanked the police.

They were walking out of Adventure World when Tess suddenly yelped.

"What's the matter?" Peter said.

Jane looked through the grass and picked up a plastic fork. "Tess stood on that," she said crossly. Jane dropped the fork in a rubbish bin.

"You'll make a great vet, Jane," Mum said. "The two of you were very kind to that lost dog too."

New Key Words

vet

Peter said, "Mum, as we love animals, could we get a pet mouse?"

"I don't think that's a good idea," said Mum.

"But they're only small," Peter pointed out.

"We've got a dog, a cat and two rabbits," said Dad. "We don't need another pet."

Looking up at the sky again, he said, "Come on. It's starting to rain."

Everyone ran home. They got inside just before the rain came down hard.

New Key Words

"We made it!" said Mum. "Much longer and we'd have been soaked. Bedtime, you two."

"Night, night," said Jane, yawning.

"Good night," Mum said.

When Peter was tucked up in bed, he said, "Mum, I'm still thinking about getting a mouse."

"Listen, Peter," Mum said, "I don't think a pet mouse is a good idea."

Peter had another idea. "Tomorrow, I'll use my pens to draw a mouse," he said.

New Key Words

The next morning, Tess was still walking around with a limp.

"We'll have to take her to the vet," Dad said.

Peter, Jane and Dad all went to the vet and sat in the waiting room.

"Look, Dad!" Peter said. "That boy by the plant has got a mouse."

"Tess," the vet shouted.

"Oh, it's our turn," Dad said, jumping up.

New Key Words

"She stood on a plastic fork," Dad told the vet. "I hope it's nothing too bad."

"Oh dear, Tess. I just need to check you over," said the vet.

The vet took a long look at Tess's paw and made some notes. "It's nothing bad," she said. "It's only a small cut. Use some of this cream on Tess's paw two times a day."

"I want to be a vet when I'm older," Jane said.

"That's a great idea!" said the vet.

New Key Words

As they left the vet, they suddenly saw their new friend.

"Jet!" Jane cried.

"Oh, hello!" said Gurdeep. "I came to get Jet checked over after his adventure. Listen, I'd like to thank you two some more. What if we all went back to Adventure World tonight, and I watched the dogs? You could go on the rides as a family."

"Oh, Dad. Could we?" cried Peter.

"That's a very good idea, Gurdeep," Dad said. "Thank you."

New Key Words

When they got home, Mum was in the garden. Dad told Mum about the visit to the vet and the plan to go back to Adventure World.

"That sounds perfect!" cried Mum. "Can someone help me with this before we go?"

She was looking at the rabbit hutch.

"We need to stop the foxes from getting in," Mum told them. "All that talk about foxes last night made me remember that we need to fix this."

Dad and Jane took Tess inside while Peter looked at the plants and helped Mum.

"Mum," he said, "I've been thinking about what you said about the mouse last night. We have the best pets in the world, so we don't need any more for a while."

"We *do* have the best pets, Peter!" Mum said, laughing. "Can you lift this for me? Now nothing can harm our rabbits."

New Key Words

"Shall we plant some food for the rabbits?" Mum said. "I have some watercress seeds."

Peter nodded. He remembered planting seeds at Aunt Liz's allotment. He took a trowel and made small holes for the seeds.

Mum looked up at the sky. "I don't think you'll need to use a watering can to water them," she said. "It looks like it will rain again."

"I hope the rain stays away for our trip to Adventure World," said Peter.

New Key Words

That night, the family went back to Adventure World.

"Adventure World is the best!" Peter said.

"This time it's even better, because Mum *and* Dad can come on the bumper cars," said Jane.

"Oh, I'm the best at these," shouted Dad, getting into a car. "You won't get around me!"

"You'll have to catch us first!" Jane cried, zooming away.

New Key Words

Answer these questions about
the story.

1 What is on the poster that Jane
spots at Adventure World?

2 What ride do Jane, Peter and Dad
go on first?

3 Why do you think Mum, Dad and
Jane shout "NO!" when Peter asks to
go on the Spooky Train ride?

4 Why do you think Jane is cross
about the plastic fork?

5 Where do Peter, Jane, Dad and Tess
go the next morning?

6 What does Gurdeep do for the
family at the end of the story?